350

Every new generation of children is enthralled by the famous stories in our Well-loved Tales series. Younger ones love to have the story read to them. Older children will enjoy the exciting stories in an easy-to-read text.

British Library Cataloguing in Publication Data
Southgate, Vera
    Rumpelstiltskin.—Rev. ed.—(Well-loved tales. Series 606D; v. 11)
    I. Title   II. Aitchison, Martin   III. Grimm,
    Jacob. Rumpelstiltskin   IV. Series
    823'.914[J]   PZ7
    ISBN 0-7214-0948-2

Revised edition
Published by Ladybird Books Ltd Loughborough Leicestershire UK
Ladybird Books Inc Lewiston Maine 04240 USA

Rumpel-stiltskin

retold by **VERA SOUTHGATE**, MA, BCom

illustrated by **MARTIN AITCHISON**

Ladybird Books

Once upon a time there was a poor miller who had one beautiful daughter.

One day the king sent for the miller. When the miller stood before the king, he was rather frightened.

Instead of remaining quiet, the foolish man said the first silly thing that popped into his head. "I have a daughter who can spin straw into gold," he said.

5

"Your daughter is indeed clever if she can do as you say!" answered the king. "Bring her to me tomorrow and we shall see."

The next day the miller took his daughter to the king's castle.

The king led the girl into a room that was almost filled with straw. The only other things in the room were a stool, a spindle and some reels.

"Now set to work," said the king, "and, if by tomorrow morning you have not spun this straw into gold, you must die."

At these words, the king left the room and locked the door behind him.

The miller's daughter sat down on the
stool and gazed at all the straw. She did
not know what to do. She had no idea
how to spin straw into gold.

As she thought about the next morning, she grew more and more afraid. At last she hid her face in her hands and wept.

All at once the door flew open and in came the strangest little man she had ever seen.

"Good evening, Mistress Miller," said the tiny man. "Why are you crying?"

"Alas!" replied the girl, "I have to

spin all this straw into gold and I do not
know how to do it."

"But I do!" said the manikin. "What will you give me if I spin it for you?"

"My necklace," replied the girl.

The little man took the necklace and sat down in front of the spinning wheel.

Whirr, whirr, whirr; three times round and one reel was full. The manikin put on another reel.

Whirr, whirr, whirr; three times round and the second reel was full. And so it went on all night.

By morning all the straw was spun and all the reels were full of gold. Whereupon the little man disappeared.

At sunrise the king arrived. He was astonished and more than delighted to see so much gold. Yet he was not satisfied. The sight of the gold only made him more greedy.

He took the miller's daughter to a second room, much larger than the first one. It, too, was full of straw.

Again the king told the girl that if all the straw was not spun into gold before next morning, she must die.

Once more, when she was left alone, the girl began to cry.

In a moment the door flew open and the manikin stood before her.

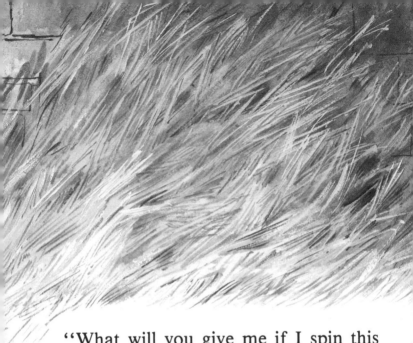

"What will you give me if I spin this straw into gold?" asked the tiny man.

"The ring on my finger," replied the miller's daughter.

The manikin took the ring and sat down before the spinning wheel. He spun straw all night until all the reels were full of gold. Then once more he disappeared.

The king arrived at sunrise and again he was delighted to see all the gold. Yet still he was not satisfied.

He led the poor girl to a third room, even larger than the other two. It, too, was full of straw.

This time the king said to the girl, "Spin this straw into gold before morning and you shall be my queen."

When the girl sat alone, weeping, the queer little man appeared for the third time.

"What will you give me if I spin the straw for you this time?" he asked.

"Alas! I have nothing more that I can give," sobbed the poor girl.

28

"Then promise me that, if you become queen, you will give me your first child," said the manikin.

"I may never become queen nor yet have a child," thought the girl. So she promised.

At that the manikin once more spun all the straw into gold.

When the king arrived, early the next morning, he was overjoyed at the sight of all the gold.

He reminded himself that, not only was the miller's daughter beautiful, but also that she had brought him great riches.

So he kept his promise. He married the

miller's daughter and she became
his queen.

The queen was very happy, living in the royal castle. She forgot all about the manikin who had spun the straw into gold.

A year after they were married, the king
and queen had a lovely baby. They were
both filled with joy.

A few days later, the manikin suddenly appeared in the queen's bedroom.

"Now give me what you promised," he said to the queen, as he pointed to the sleeping baby.

The poor queen was horrified and clutched her baby tightly to her.

The queen offered the manikin all the riches of her kingdom, if only he would release her from her promise.

The tiny man refused them all. "A human child would be dearer to me than all the riches of your kingdom," he said to the queen.

At his words, the poor queen wept so
bitterly, that the tiny man took pity on her.

"I will give you three days," he said,
"and if in that time you can guess my
name, you shall keep your child."

That night the queen lay awake, trying

to remember every name she had ever
heard.

In the morning the queen sent for a messenger. She told him to ride all over the country, collecting all the boys' names he could find.

When the little man came the next day, the queen repeated her long list of names. But after each name the manikin said, "No, that is not my name."

The next morning the queen sent out
her messenger to another country. He
came back with a long list of the queerest

names she had ever heard.

The queen repeated all these strange names to the little man, on his second visit. After each name he shook his head and said, "No, that is not my name."

The poor queen was in despair.

On the third day, it was very late when the messenger returned.

"I have not been able to find one new name," he said, "but, as I came to a high mountain, at the end of the forest, I saw a little house. In front of the house, a fire was burning.

"The queerest little man was hopping and jumping round the fire," went on the messenger, "and this is what he was singing:

Although today I brew and bake,
Tomorrow the queen's own child I'll take.
This guessing game she'll never win,
For my name is Rumpelstiltskin."

On hearing this, the queen clapped her hands with joy.

When the manikin arrived, she pretended she still did not know his name.

"Is your name Twinkletoes?" she asked.

"No, that is not my name," he replied.

"Is it Shagribanda?" she asked.

"No, that is not my name," he replied.

"Does it happen to be Rumpel-stiltskin?"

The manikin was furious. "A witch has told you! A witch has told you!" he shrieked, as he stamped his foot in anger.

He stamped so hard that his right leg

went through the floor. At that, his anger increased. He seized his leg with both hands and began to pull with all his might. He pulled so hard that at last his leg came out of the hole.

Then Rumpelstiltskin stumped furiously out of the room and was never heard of again.